What's the Matter, Little Frog?

By Lucille Hammond

Illustrated by
Maggie Swanson

RANDOM HOUSE 🏠 NEW YORK

Text copyright © 1987 by Lucille Hammond. Illustrations copyright © 1987 by Maggie Swanson. All rights reserved under International and Pan-American Copyright Conventions. Published in the United States by Random House, Inc., New York, and simultaneously in Canada by Random House of Canada Limited, Toronto. ISBN: 0-394-88865-0 Library of Congress Catalog Card Number: 86-22081 Manufactured in Singapore
1 2 3 4 5 6 7 8 9 0

Little Frog felt sad one day, and he began to cry.
His tears fell into the water and floated across the
pond to a rock where a wise duck sat resting.

"Someone is crying," said Duck. And off she
swam to see what was going on.

She soon found Little Frog.
"What's the matter, Little Frog?"
asked Duck. "Why are you crying?"
"I don't know," said Little Frog.
"Could it be," said Duck,
"that you are lost and cannot find
your pond?"

"Oh, no," said Little Frog. "This is my pond, and I like it very much."
Duck shook her head because she could not think of any other reason.
"Let's ask someone else," she said.

So off they went, Little Frog jumping and Duck waddling, up the path and into the woods.

They soon met a cheerful squirrel.

"Hello, Squirrel," said Duck. "Little Frog is sad,
and he doesn't know why."

Squirrel looked at Little Frog.

"Could it be," said Squirrel, "that you are hungry
and need something to eat?"

"Oh, no," said Little Frog. "I have just had my
lunch, and I am not hungry."

Squirrel shook his head because he could not think of any other reason. "Let's ask someone else," he said.

So off they went, Little Frog jumping and Duck waddling, up the path and through the woods, and Squirrel went with them, running along.

They soon met a friendly snake.

"Hello, Snake," said Duck. "Little Frog is sad, and he doesn't know why."

Snake looked at Little Frog.

"Could it be," said Snake, "that you have no place to live and need a home?"

"Oh, no," said Little Frog. "I have a home, and it is just right for me."

Snake shook his head because he could not think of any other reason.

"Let's ask someone else," he said.

So off they went, Little Frog jumping and Duck waddling and Squirrel running, up the path and through the woods, and Snake went with them, slithering along.

They soon met a curious fox.

"Hello, Fox," said Duck. "Little Frog is sad, and he doesn't know why."

Fox looked at Little Frog.

"Could it be," said Fox, "that your mother and father have gone away and left you behind?"

"Oh, no," said Little Frog. "My mother and father are at home, and they will be glad to see me when I get back."

Fox shook her head because she could not think of any other reason.

"Let's ask someone else," she said.

So off they went, Little Frog jumping and Duck waddling and Squirrel running and Snake slithering, up the path and through the woods, and Fox went with them, ambling along.

They soon met a clever mouse.

"Hello, Mouse," said Duck. "Little Frog is sad, and he doesn't know why."

Mouse looked at Little Frog.

"Could it be," said Mouse, "that you are lonely and need someone to play with?"

Little Frog thought for a moment and then he cried, "Oh, yes! That's it! I am lonely and need someone to play with."

"Well," said Mouse. "I think I know a way to help you."

She scampered off and soon returned with a large
piece of cardboard and a big crayon.

"I'll make a sign and everyone can read it," she said.

Mouse wrote some words on the cardboard.

Then she held up the sign so that everyone could read it. The sign said LITTLE FROG NEEDS A FRIEND.

"Wait just a minute!" said the wise duck. "I'll be your friend, Little Frog."

"So will I!" said the cheerful squirrel.

"So will I!" said the friendly snake.

"So will I!" said the curious fox.

"So will I!" said the clever mouse.

Little Frog was so happy, he could hardly believe it.
Now he had five wonderful friends.

"What a lucky frog I am!" he said. "Who wants to
play with me down by the pond?"

So off they went, Little Frog jumping and
Duck waddling and Squirrel running and
Snake slithering and Fox ambling, down the
path and back to the pond, and Mouse went
with them, scampering along.